Dandelion Ghosts

and other stories

Jen Knox

Unleash PRESS

Published by Unleash Press

Reynoldsburg, OH 43068

unleashcreatives.net/press

Copyright © 2021 by Jen Knox

Illustrations by Christopher Shanahan

Printed in the United States of America

Dedication

This book is dedicated to all those who inspired or supported the individual works. Thank you to Domi J. Shoemaker, Carol Fischbach and the rest of the corporeal community for offering the springboard for many of these pieces. Heartfelt gratitude to the Flash Fiction Magazine team. Gratitude-filled shout outs go to friends and editors extraordinaire, Rebecca Grubb and Cindy Hochman, who teach me many things about the mechanics of language that I perpetually forget. Finally, thank you to Chris Shanahan who made this book and much of my life a thing of beauty.

Dandelion Ghosts

Contents

Dandelion Ghosts

We were born into curiosity and raised with a light touch. We ran around trees and chased ice cream trucks down the street or stared at the world through cameras and recorded what we saw in bound journals.

The crumbling concrete alongside our homes led to narrow alleyways that promised adulthood. We congregated on the summer solstice, the longest day of the year, and marched past the plump blackberry vines and fields of dandelions. Stopping to taste the fruit or flick the heads of flowers into the alley, we enjoyed the last bit of childhood beneath a blue sky. Dirty fingers and playful shoves.

Once beyond the fields, the awkwardness and delights of youth would be over, and the mysteries that awaited would be revealed. We couldn't wait to solve the riddle that stumped so many before us.

No one sat on back porches to monitor our pace or offer words of wisdom. The elders were too tired. The homes we left were perpetual rehab projects, tall and brick. There was nothing alluring to make us turn around. There were no home-cooked meals or promises of stories at night. The basements held ghosts and dust. The mistakes of those who came before us.

Just before we reached adulthood, the vines became thicker. Blackberries covered the path, either smashed or whole. Small animals watched and waited till there was stillness as, one by one, we reached the end of the alley, where the riddle was presented to us at last. There must be rules to freedom and ambiguity around structure.

A simple sign directed us. Move forward to trade, go uphill to give, run downhill to take. We scattered, some going on instinct, while others turned back after a headlong dash.

Beyond the signs were homes like those we grew up in, only made with solar panels. Wind turbines overlooked our town, and the air was clean. We found the homes we liked the best and began to fill our roles: providing, taking and exchanging what we found at hand. We ate berries and harvested dandelions for tea and medicine. Some ate rabbit and racoon, while others chewed on bark and plucked tiny insects to bake into brownies.

The first decade of adulthood, the majority decided to provide. We grew strong and steady like the rivers where we caught fish and swam every solstice. Our celebrations were boisterous, and our rest was deep. But some of us grew bored and began to take unapologetically. The trend continued until there was more need for exchange.

We changed roles again after a few years, or a few realizations. Takers found guilt and opulence alike; providers smiled wearily while worrying over time and lack of resources. Those responsible for exchanging goods were always counting, and this drove most to madness.

The second decade, takers demanded more homes and stockpiled fish. Those who traded were told what to say, and we began to look at each other with wariness. The few providers starved; some died and were buried in basements, where our children would play with their ghosts.

The path toward death was a circle. We walked it until we grew too tired, and then we watched as our children moved away. They skipped toward a lake where they would create a new life.

They took a path worn into the fields that were full of soy and marigolds, and they ended up who knows where, with new signs. We watched as our parents had, talking to our ghosts, asking them what comes next, and they told us to wait.

The children approached their riddle. One sign told them to look inward, another outward, and yet a third to look directly up.

We watched as their heads moved. Some closed their eyes, while others examined the earth, and those who remained pointed upwards toward the stars. We watched them for decades.

Though some never moved, others refused to sit still, and those looking up imposed stories they couldn't prove; we swelled with pride. Their riddle was tougher than ours, and we applauded their hardscrabble journey.

As our children walked in circles, their children shook their heads and made their way toward another life; new ghosts remained. And we began to band together to move beyond brick and basement, stone and soy, to create new riddles for all the children as they rushed and argued, created and destroyed, and ultimately found out how little they knew.

Trickster

The animal who lives in her lower ribcage chitters, trying to get her to play; it loves nothing more than to distract from rational thought. She chuckled knowingly the first time she heard the phrase "monkey mind" because squirrels are worse. They're tricksters.

She feeds and cares for her squirrel. Bob Ross would be proud. She feeds it neurosis and sugar, lots of sugar, until the day she thinks something needs to change. When she gives the eviction notice, the squirrel laughs before burrowing in her ribcage and curling into a tight little ball. She stretches and shoves it down with diaphragmatic breath. But it climbs higher and settles in again, explaining that tricksters are closest to God.

When one is liberated, what else is there to do but play?

Seeking support, she travels, but her spirit guides and gurus become restless because she never fully listens. The medicines they offer are always clear and delivered with precise instructions, step-by-step guides. But medicine piles up in her cupboards, not her body. In the body, it might take over.

She believes that in a decade or two, we will have the information we need to control our own thoughts without relying on discipline. We can almost do it now, but not quite. Not without side effects. She tells the squirrel this, says that she can see a future in which she will control everything, and it will fade from existence with a single intentional breath.

If I disappear, what will be left?

She imagines staring out the window, watching the willow oaks sway and mourning doves bound gently in her yard as a sunrise fills the world with the perfect balance of light and color. She imagines being immersed in this perfection and seeing nothing ahead of or behind her. In this image, she feels nothing.

She continues to feed her squirrel. She can easily feed it for the rest of her life. She has a backpack full of dramas from the past in case she runs out of neurosis. The squirrel likes this. It likes the churn. Its mad frenetic energy lives near enough her heart to keep her dangerous. Just dangerous enough to do things in the world.

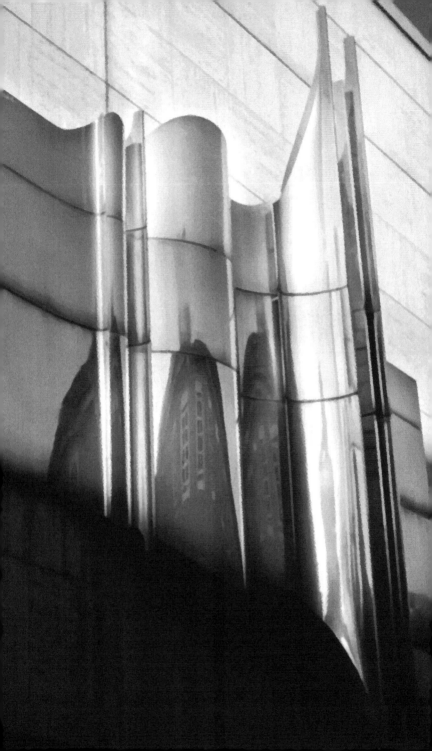

The Meaning of Life

Shortly before Leo died, he became like art himself. Still and reflective, he emanated peace. I slid my finger across my phone screen, showing him pictures of an exhibition for the city, and he attempted a weak laugh. "Remember the potholes?"

I placed his hand on my belly. "I do."

In 2008, Leo and I were hired by a lottery-ticket millionaire who found our business card on a table at a Korean restaurant in the middle of a strip mall in rural Indiana. He asked us to create an elaborate and near-impossible mirror waterfall sculpture right next to a dollar store. This is what it meant to make money as an artist.

When he hired us, the lottery-ticket millionaire told the story of getting two teeth knocked out near that very same stretch of cracked asphalt and gravel. He said it was the ugliest part of his hometown. We built the polarity of his experience by digging deep into the ground, working with a construction team to remove gravel and dirt and fill the space with a mosaic of cobalt and silver ceramic and glass.

It was a big break for semi-professional installation artists who had quit their day jobs, and the outlandishness of it helped to offset our missteps. Leo's friends and former construction site co-workers hauled supplies and broke ground, but when it came to the actual art installation, we were on our own. We couldn't figure out how to turn the sketch I'd made of mirror pools and a backlit waterfall magnified by meticulously placed ceramic shards into reality.

Multiple times that last month, drivers seeking cheap dish detergent sacrificed tires to the treacherous dollar store parking lot. I made large motions with my arms to direct the traffic away from potholes, but no one paid attention, and no one seemed to care what we were doing, only what was being done. By the time a young girl ran toward us from the passenger's side door of a rusty CRX to examine our work, we were almost finished, and I invited her to stand where I stood.

"It's like another world," she said.

The girl's mother tugged her away, leaving us with an admonishing glare, but we stood a little taller. We'd pulled it off. I cupped my belly and glanced down to whisper. Leo placed his hand on mine as we relished in the success of this odd legacy project that, to us, led somewhere new. The elegance of the waterfall urged us to displace belief forever.

When the lottery-ticket millionaire met us at the unveiling, he examined the ceramic labyrinth slowly. "It beckons people with its what-the-fuck mantra to walk with peace," I told him. He slapped me on the back, probably harder than he intended, then held up a hand to high-five Leo.

"Hell yeah!" he said. A decent first review. It was five years before meth addicts destroyed it.

Ten years later, Leo and I were commissioned to build an adult-size playground on the top of a skyscraper hotel that included a slide that left its rider on a soft couch near a private bar. This was when we decided to quit taking such jobs. At least, we decided this after signing the sizable contract that would pay our rent for six months.

Twin brothers with balding heads aimed to have bikini-clad women who were, like them, bored by abundance, land in their laps. They were recapturing their youth, they admitted with ironic laughter.

"10-4," I said, handing them a sketch.

Four days into the project, Leo placed his hand on my belly and asked it how to make meaning of life. Despite this tender moment, Leo was no longer my husband, and I had taken to calling him Leonardo, which made him buy a blue bandana and sometimes call me "dude."

I augmented a hand-tufted white leather couch for the brothers by adding hydraulics, and we collected a check.

When I first met Leo, thirteen years ago, he was on site with a couple dozen other construction workers in hardhats. I approached him, and as I did, I held my belly as though protecting it. He watched as though he too could hear her speak.

We got a drink on a Saturday after I asked for his number. Months passed during which we sketched ideas on each other's bodies, daydreamed about owning a business, living as artists. We fed off each other's energy and inspiration. Leo learned to dance with and befriend my muse, his ear glued to my navel.

In 2020, Leo became sick along with the country, the world. We landed a job to create a sculpture of children holding hands, of adults in masks, of a rainbow that spread out over the bronze statues to reflect the light. I was on my own.

I had never worked on my own with the contractors, and they were initially disrespectful. So I matched their rudeness, which made them reverent. I held the soft flesh of my belly and asked it what to do right in front of these men, and they listened as deeply as I did.

People walked by with itchy masks hiding irritated bumps. They argued near busses and griped about the restrictions or the lack there-of. But one of the figures seemed to straddle the world. She held a slightly swollen belly that was full of hope, and she was where people paused.

Leo and I had been easily distracted before he became ill. We'd been unable to slow down enough to sit for a full meal. There was too much to observe and create, so much so that we were never home. That is, until quarantine brought us together. The world, the illness and proximity, compressed us to the point of purity.

I leaned in as Leo whispered, "We just need to stay still long enough to understand." I felt the roughness of his beard and softened to match it. I pushed my belly to his. We both listened for the faint heartbeat and asked it to guide us. It did more than that.

Dandelion Ghosts

Lions

At thirty-six, Lee could barely make rent. The swell of a newly pollinated spring day caught in her ribs as she and her partner, Kai, recited their morning affirmations for wealth and abundance. They watered the marigolds that lived in their balcony garden.

Lee repeated the affirmations every time she needed to ignore the better rehearsed mantras in her head about how all the monied are corrupt. It was a deeply embedded program that she blamed on her father who would spend more than he made proudly, using the word *current* when he spoke of currency, saying it needed to flow.

"There's no t," Lee had argued then, confused by his aversion to savings accounts.

Her father assured her that he knew what he was doing. Her childhood home might have been falling apart, but the collection of ivory pipes her father kept on the mantel would've easily covered the mortgage for two months. The couch her father had cobbled together from old upholstery, springs, wood beams and pillows provided painful support, whereas the family ate dinner at an invaluable handcrafted table adorned with the faces of lions so ornate that they were bound to one day come to life. And so, they did.

Just before Lee and Kai were about to be evicted, the lions arrived. The windfall they brought on their backs blew heavy air into the open windows. The knuckled paws rapped late at night. Lee was surprised the creatures wanted to stay in such modest conditions, but she made space on the living room floor. Kai stroked their manes.

Soon after the arrival, the flow of money became steadier. Lee had the foresight to open an online shop to supplement an unexpected dip in sales at the metaphysical store they owned. Online, the couple sold candles and oils, and Lee was surprised that a simple posting on her social channels led to enough sales to pay the rent.

When Kai started printing brown, lettered labels in the garage, things picked up more.

The soy candle labels promised to burn all bad luck within months or bring abundance in seven days. Lee melted the wax in a double boiler, poured it with love and a handful of herbs, maybe even a crystal or two. She included kind notes, a blessing or prayer, and the lions would hold the wick as they waited for the wax to solidify.

The emails of gratitude and pleas for advice began to pour in, and Lee answered each one the best she could. She offered the wisdom others had offered her. Or the wisdom she wished others had offered her. She told her new electronic pen pals to trust their intuition, to look for the question not the answer, to tune in and reach out.

There were money manifestation questions that she answered with her own story of abundance, new as it was, and the promise that if it could happen for her it could happen for anyone. Her authenticity cut through, and every now and then someone would follow up with a new order and a story of success.

Lee lit candle after candle, watching the fire. When orders exceeded capacity, she knew they'd need to move, but the lions refused. They would stay in this small apartment in southern Ohio and bless the next person with wealth; they could only take this couple so far. Lee asked if they'd helped her father, and they refused to answer.

Lee remembered her mother's sadness those last nights. Her father had spent rent money again to create a giant sculpture he called "Muffler Woman." The sculpture itself was just a bunch of old rusted metal with a muffler for pelvic support, but the soldering iron and time he took away from more commercial projects cost them all healthy food for months. Still young enough to enjoy living on a diet of hot dogs and ramen, Lee tried to tune out the fights as the house turned gray and the flower wallpaper began to pollinate, suffocating them all.

She spoke to her mother every weekend but hadn't seen her father in years. She'd tried to reach out a few times, believed he lived near the corner stores that were in walking distance of the art shops, where he used to paint faces for tips. Her mother worried he was homeless.

The last time Lee saw her father, he had a new tattoo of a ram on his bicep, which he flexed proudly as he walked her to his latest creation: a blown glass spiral that he said represented time.

When the business demanded they leave the apartment, Lee tracked her father down and found out that he did, in fact, stay in a warehouse-turned apartment complex. She called his landlord to prepay his rent, hoping if nothing else for peace of mind. But the landlord told her that her father was already ahead on rent and trying to buy the building. "That man has this crazy idea that he can build up and turn this into an artist residency taller than any skyscraper, like a beanstalk," he keeps saying, "I worry about him sometimes."

Lee waited for more steady information, but it didn't come. "In that case, please have him call me."

He never called, but Lee found out that his paintings were now selling for triple what they once did. When Lee's father died, there was no money and no debt. There was no will. "I don't live in future tense," he once said.

What her father left instead was a compact pile of frenetic energy that she swooped up and kept in a small ivory box next to the pipes, which lived on a windowsill in her beautiful home near the woods.

Lee and Kai were kind to their neighbors. Kai planted marigold and snapdragon seeds in the front yard as Lee answered letters, both those of thanks and those that accused her of running scams. "I paid fourteen dollars for this prosperity candle, and I'm poorer than ever," one said. To each email, letter and review, Lee tried her best to offer reassurances, but she was finding it harder to be empathetic.

"To get what you expect might be a disappointment, but to get what you want is terrifying," she told a particularly dubious customer. When Kai nudged her late nights, asking, "You there?" As she worked on business plans to expand, she would find a moment to reflect on her mother's sadness.

To move with the currency of life is to forget to stay still. At thirty-nine, Lee summoned the lions.

Instead of arriving, they sent only their roar. The pipes began to smoke themselves, and the rhythm of life continued as Lee blew out candles and joined her husband on the patio, where they marveled at the marigolds beginning to bloom.

Popliteal Fossa

Money was born at the backs of her knees. As a young girl she stumbled, and the coins piled up beneath her heels. It was a neat trick that caused her parents to sing the girl's praises before making their demands and, ultimately, trying to rip from her what they couldn't see. When the coins were all used up, they disappeared.

As an older child, she traversed her coastal city with a slanty-headed green toy made of clay that could bend to accommodate any circumstance. This toy, a gift from her late grandmother, taught her to worship asymmetrical things. She saw the world as a splendor of odd shapes and, as she got older, learned to avoid mirrors and people with pretty faces.

As a young adult, she walked the beaches alone and wanted nothing. She found a stretch of sand to settle on, but those who shared the land were fierce. They'd steal anything they could from her body and her bags, but they didn't know what to do with what they stole.

Now with nothing, she slept on the warm sand, sober, while those nearby bought things to smoke or imbibe or dissolve on their tongues. As these substances dissolved them in turn, she learned to offer compassion from afar. Knowing about the soft spot at the backs of her knees, she waited until the sun fell and journeyed onward.

On an indigo night, she walked toward a beach that had a sign saying "no textiles," a term that nudists used to describe the clothed. It seemed a fitting place to camp. The first few nights, she saw too much flesh too fast. After a while, however, she found delight in their awkwardness, the scattershot parts that made up the machines. They were all machines, barely working, but honest about it.

A seeker, she continued to move, until she found an expanse that called to her. Flowers blossomed from the hands of one beach dweller, while another worshiped the water-heavy sand as it fell in clumps from his fingers. Home. Wading into the water, she knocked her knees together for the first time in years, filling the hidden corners of the ocean with coins.

At one time, she thought she was broken, shattered like a piggy bank. Her parents and others had cut themselves on her edges. But knowing how to lose it all only to discover there's nothing to lose, she learned to trade starfish for seashells, and only fleetingly wondered where the coins would surface. At the mouth of the ocean, each night, she created more than the entire world could spend and, as others explored their freedoms and greed, she wished them all well.

Retirement

I'm having second thoughts. The stone statue of Themis takes on a blue hue in this light. Beneath a deep orange sky, her scales are unbalanced after a summer of crime. She and I stand above a slate gray building where I've worked as a judge for over twenty years.

Moral and natural justice used to feel like the same thing, until one day they didn't. I used to want to save the world.

"I'm tired," I tell her.

Her face is both stoic and determined. As a breeze causes the little hairs on my arms to ripple, I sit by her feet. On the rooftop, we stare at those entering and leaving the courthouse as the earthy colors blend ground and sky. I once read that to cultivate stillness one need only to look straight ahead for long enough. No wavering. Everything that happens in the periphery will bow to this focus.

My eyes are like lasers, until the light blurs and scatters. A young boy looks up, and instead of worry crossing his face, he waves. Instead of waving back, I think of Dee. We weren't supposed to be friends.

Her heart broke when a kid she'd defended went on to kill both of his parents. Before she retired, we would sit here with the goddess in fold-out chairs and dream about an ideal world, one that only created. She'd paint her claw-like nails the color of strawberry taffy as I bounced my knee nervously, agonizing over the next right question to ask. I wanted to offer her comfort, to know that the ideal was possible.

Optimism allowed me to absorb more than most because those on trial couldn't. Or didn't. And that's the thing with energy, it embeds itself somewhere and either collects or flows. The denser it is, the more likely it will crawl behind

your shoulder blades rendering wings static. Dee
used to listen to me say such things and tell me
that I was the reason she drank, not the juvenile
offenders she represented. This made us laugh.

A small pile of crisp leaves collects on the roof, so
I slide off my flats and step one bare foot on the
pile, then the other, nestling my toes into the crisp
fragile leaves. Standing there on a pile near
Themis, I notice she is no longer facing me but
seemingly watching the swirl from a towering oak
nearby.

A year ago, I spread ashes at the base of that oak.
Now, Dee lives in the stipules that reach out as
the wind carries. I imagine her here, speaking
more clearly to the goddess who is giving up on
me the way I am giving up on justice. Dee had
been the one to protest and fight, to model all
forms of justice I knew.

But as sky caramelizes and the sun sets, I know
it's time. The last time. With leaf debris still in my
toes, I put on my shoes and glance at the scales
the goddess Themis carries. I stare with focus as
the peripheral scene fills with victims—criminals

and witnesses move briskly toward their cars as reds and browns adorn the earth and the swirl of wind insists on breaking the pattern of gravity. I watch as the sun falls.

A young woman in the court's parking lot runs to an elderly woman, and they embrace. Their tears summon a hard but brief rain that softens everything and everyone. I embrace each tear falling from the sky and soften. The blue goddess softens as well, reminding me what autumn reminds us all. "Death is the marker of a long life," an old Irish saying goes.

I fold this promise into each step forward, and I listen as the scales begin to recalibrate. I listen as the cars come and go, each containing a story of crime and sentencing or acquittal, each containing a story too complex to call. I hold my badge tightly as I slip back into the building and down the stairs, out the door and to a car of my own. I never look back.

Dandelion Ghosts

Lottery Days

You told me not to play with matches that
summer, so I palmed a corner-store lighter
instead. The flame reached for the tip of your
blue Crayon, until you knocked the lighter from
my hands. You wanted to color the sky, you said,
and I wouldn't ruin your chance.

I plodded behind, watching socks fall down the
backs of your ankles. You explained that this is
why we shouldn't buy socks at Odd Lots, which
was sometimes Big Lots, because kids knew. Feet
knew. The store carried three coat styles, and
mine was one. I liked the color for fall, a warm
maroon. You tugged at the longer sleeve.

We were both coupled by winter, our hearts twisted like tree trunks. We ate cold shrimp in the living room of a one-bedroom apartment near downtown, watching Power Puff Girls and retelling jokes, adjusting bra straps and headbands, discussing jobs that allowed money of our own. We quantified everything those lottery days, green grapes or tiramisu.

We were plump like prunes that spring, tired of snow. Grown. Perhaps this is why I chose to move somewhere warm. Heart still twisted, I navigated a state that you had stitched atop a heart on a pillow that I hugged like a tiny person. I told you I had a black thumb, a fun term for not understanding the relentlessness of a southern sun. You said talking to plants gives them life, not because they hear you but because they feed on your breath. It doesn't matter why a thing works, so long as it does.

I never told you that I kept the garden for you, a swell of life that you will never see. We never admitted such sentimental things. But it's here now, your garden. It thrives for you beneath a sometimes-blue sky.

Dandelion Ghosts

Áine

As I ease down, shedding the heat, my sits bones feel like ball bearings on the cold floor. Some people here glow. Others are dull. A young woman directs us to breathe, and her voice reverberates like a tuning fork.

I can already hear the bombardment of sound I'll soon absorb. My husband is sitting at the piano slamming keys, when I open the door. My mother-in-law, who lives two houses down, will holler when she sees me. They'll accuse me of relapsing, like I did last time I disappeared. It's been three weeks.

The percentage of time I spent away is miniscule really, but they don't understand time in this way.

What they'll have the most trouble understanding is that I left nearly naked in the middle of an Ohio cold snap, after waking from a dead sleep. I left the way they warn might happen when taking over-the-counter sleeping pills, but I wasn't on pills. I was as clear as I'd ever been.

What beckoned me was a crackling beneath the ground, a call to fire. I ran to the trees to barter with them, to breathe deeper, to bathe in the forest. It was glorious, until I lost all sensation and noticed I wasn't alone. There were others, wandering but not lost, like the bumper sticker on Mom's battered Volvo used to say. They did not speak, did not hold shape, but our energy fused, and together we created light.

We lit up the world for days, diffusing the storm and eradicating disease. The illumination was what we were called to do. When the light was no longer needed, I returned. Clothed in a loose-fitting top and jeans, I found myself in front of a run-down church where homeless people come to participate in free meditation sessions.

I sit with them all now, and I feel both freedom and burden. After a few breaths, I get up and walk out. When I arrive home, my husband looks at me as though I've tried to steal his life, but his brow softens when I reach out my arms.

"The storm, Áine," he says. His throat is dry. He doesn't drink enough water, doesn't get enough sun. When I'm away, he stays indoors, pacing, waiting.

"Yes," I say.

"We thought you'd freeze to death." His breath is warm.

The mother-in-law is on her way. Before I am bombarded with noise, funneled into a hospital room and fed medications that I don't need, medications that cannot touch my radiance, I embrace my husband. I forgive him.

I tighten my grip, trying to tell him all I know— teeth grazing the tiny hairs on his ear. And when he kisses my forehead with genuine apology, I infuse him with light. Our thoughts solidify just before the rest of life barges in.

Some say I'm delusional. I am ignored and fed new combinations of "cures," but nothing they can give me will keep me dull for long. As the world darkens, I wait for the opportunity to be called. To light it up again.

Dandelion Ghosts

Dandelion Ghosts

Troika

The silver and turquoise ring I bought at a community festival isn't quite right for any one of my fingers. Too loose on my ring finger, suffocates my index, and to wear a ring on one's middle finger, I hear, is like inviting the chaos of the universe into your life.

I wear the turquoise snugly. It protects me from a salt-heavy diet. It tells me when I'm in the luteal phase of my menstrual cycle. I can even gauge humidity when it's stuck. I've read stories about rings getting jammed on fingers, squeezing flesh and having to be cut off. I sometimes imagine the horror of this scene.

The turquoise is in the shape of an elongated oval with a thick band, and it'd be a bitch to cut free. And yet. I wear this ring when I teach. I like the way it clangs against the others as I rub my hands together. I like the way it reminds me of my grandmother's hands, which were so delicate yet sure of themselves and always adorned in turquoise.

The stone represents balance, voice and calm; though I never saw evidence of that in my grandmother, I do not dismiss anything. I've learned that to dismiss a thing is to make it disappear. It's the one trick all humans use to their own detriment.

I always wonder about the peddlers of anything, but I took particular interest in the ring peddler I met last summer because he had passion. When I tried on the ring, he simply nodded and suggested a guard. It wasn't until I told him my intent to purchase for the sticker price of thirty-two dollars that he told me of its magnificence. He said he'd hand-selected this stone from a dozen based on the subtle vibration he felt in his palm when he first felt its weight.

I told him "Thank you. Someone should make a Netflix special about you."

Everyone deserves their own Netflix special, but especially ring peddlers. Years ago, I sold rings in a department store. I only stole one, but it was gaudy and old—something no one would buy at that store but the pawn shop welcomed. It paid the rent. I never got caught but sometimes timelines are off, and I was sure I'd had my teeth knocked in by that event years prior.

Often, in that store, I made a practice of picking up ordinary, overpriced items and asking them what they promised. A decorative stone spoke of grounding, a pair of socks offered comfort, the entire makeup aisle vowed enchantment, and a self-help book dispensed cheap wisdom.

Not all rings have an offering, or their offering expires. I wear a troika of them. That means three in Russian. I'm four percent Russian. Three horses at the front of a carriage remind me to lead with my hands, then my heart, then my head.

I no longer steal. I no longer prepay for future bullshit. I wear the turquoise often. When I rotate it, I imagine the planets and their chaos. When it's too tight, I wait it out. I wonder about the ring peddler's newest finds, but I don't visit him again. It's good to know when you have enough.

List of Illustrations

Acknowledgements

"The Meaning of Life" appears in *The New Guard Volume X*, "Lottery Days" originally appeared in *Literary Orphans* and was reprinted in *The Best Small Fictions*, and "Trickster" was originally published in *MoonPark Review*, "Lions" appears in *Emerge Literary Journal*, and "Dandelion Ghosts" and "Popliteal Fossa" were both published in *Flash Fiction Magazine*. "Dandelion Ghosts" was the 2020 Flash Fiction Contest Winner.

Made in the USA
Columbia, SC
19 February 2022

56491167R00035